Best Book of Princess Stories

Miles Kelly

First published in 2018 by Miles Kelly Publishing Ltd
Harding's Barn, Bardfield End Green, Thaxted, Essex, CM6 3PX, UK

2 4 6 8 10 9 7 5 3 1

Publishing Director Belinda Gallagher
Creative Director   Jo Cowan
Editorial Director   Rosie Neave
Design Manager   Joe Jones
Production Elizabeth Collins, Jennifer Brunwin-Jones
Reprographics Stephan Davis, Jennifer Cozens
Assets Lorraine King

ISBN 978-1-78617-522-9

Printed in China

British Library Cataloguing-in-Publication Data
A catalogue record for this book is available from the British Library

ACKNOWLEDGEMENTS
The publishers would like to thank the following artists who have contributed to this book:
Louise Wright at Plum Pudding Illustration Agency (The Twelve Dancing Princesses)
Kim Barnes at The Bright Agency (Rapunzel)
Sarah Jennings at The Bright Agency (Beauty and the Beast)
Alex Willmore at Astound (The Frog Prince)

Made with paper from a sustainable forest

www.mileskelly.net

The Twelve Dancing Princesses

There was once a king who had twelve daughters. They slept in twelve beds in one big room.

When the princesses went to bed each night, the king locked their door.

4

But each morning the king unlocked the door to find the princesses' shoes completely worn out.

It was as if they had been dancing all night.

So the king set a challenge. If a young man could discover where the princesses went at night, he could choose one to be his wife.

6

Many accepted the challenge. They were given a room next to the princesses' chamber.

But every young man failed to stay awake. Each morning there was yet another pile of worn-out shoes.

A soldier passing by heard about the king's challenge. "I would like to marry a princess," he said.

Suddenly an old woman appeared.

"When the eldest princess offers you some wine, just pretend to drink it. For in it is a sleeping powder."

The woman gave the soldier a magic cloak. "This will make you invisible, so you can follow the princesses."

At the castle, the soldier was shown to his room.

When the eldest princess gave him some wine, he tipped it away. Then he lay down and pretended to fall asleep.

The princesses dressed in dancing gowns and shoes. Then they opened a secret trapdoor and crept down the stairs.

The soldier put on the magic cloak and became invisible. He unlocked the door and followed the youngest princess down the stairs.

12

They came to a wood of golden trees. The soldier broke off a branch to take back to the king.

"Someone is following us!" said the youngest princess, but her sisters just laughed at her.

13

Then they came to a lake, upon which were twelve boats. In each boat was a handsome prince, waiting for a princess.

The soldier slipped onto the same boat as the youngest princess.

The princes rowed across the lake to a shining castle. Then they all went into the castle, followed by the soldier.

Inside, the sound of trumpets, horns and drums could be heard. The princesses began to dance with their princes.

The invisible soldier tried to dance too.

The princesses became
thirsty, but whenever they
lifted a glass to drink, the
soldier drank the glass dry.

The youngest princess
was very frightened.

17

The princesses danced and danced,
and did not stop until 3 o'clock in
the morning, when their shoes
were quite worn out.

19

They rowed back across the lake.
This time the soldier sat in the boat
with the eldest princess.

When the princesses arrived back in their chamber, they kicked off their worn-out shoes and fell fast asleep.

21

That morning, the king called for the soldier to have breakfast with him.

"Have you discovered where my daughters go and what they do?"

22

"Yes," said the soldier, and he showed the king the gold branch he had hidden under his magic cloak. He told the king exactly what he had seen.

"Wake the princesses!" the king cried.

Soon twelve sleepy princesses were stood in front of their father.

When they saw the gold branch, they had no choice but to tell the truth.

24

"Which princess would you like to marry?" asked the king. "The eldest princess," said the soldier. They were married that day.

25

The princess taught the soldier how to dance, and they lived happily ever after.

Rapunzel

Once there was a man and a woman who lived in a lovely cottage. It was perfect, except for one thing...

...their neighbour was a powerful witch.

28

One day the couple found out that they were going to have a baby. They set to work to get the nursery ready.

The room had a view of the witch's splendid garden.

One day the woman
saw the most delicious-
looking lettuce growing
in the witch's garden.

It looked so fresh and green
that she longed to eat it.

Days passed, and she could think of nothing else. She became pale and thin. Her husband cooked yummy meals, but the food tasted like ashes in her mouth.

31

The man was very worried about his wife. So that night he climbed over the high wall into the witch's garden. But as soon as he grabbed the lettuce a voice rang out,

"How dare you steal from me!"

The man stuttered that he had been afraid his wife would die if she could not eat the lettuce.

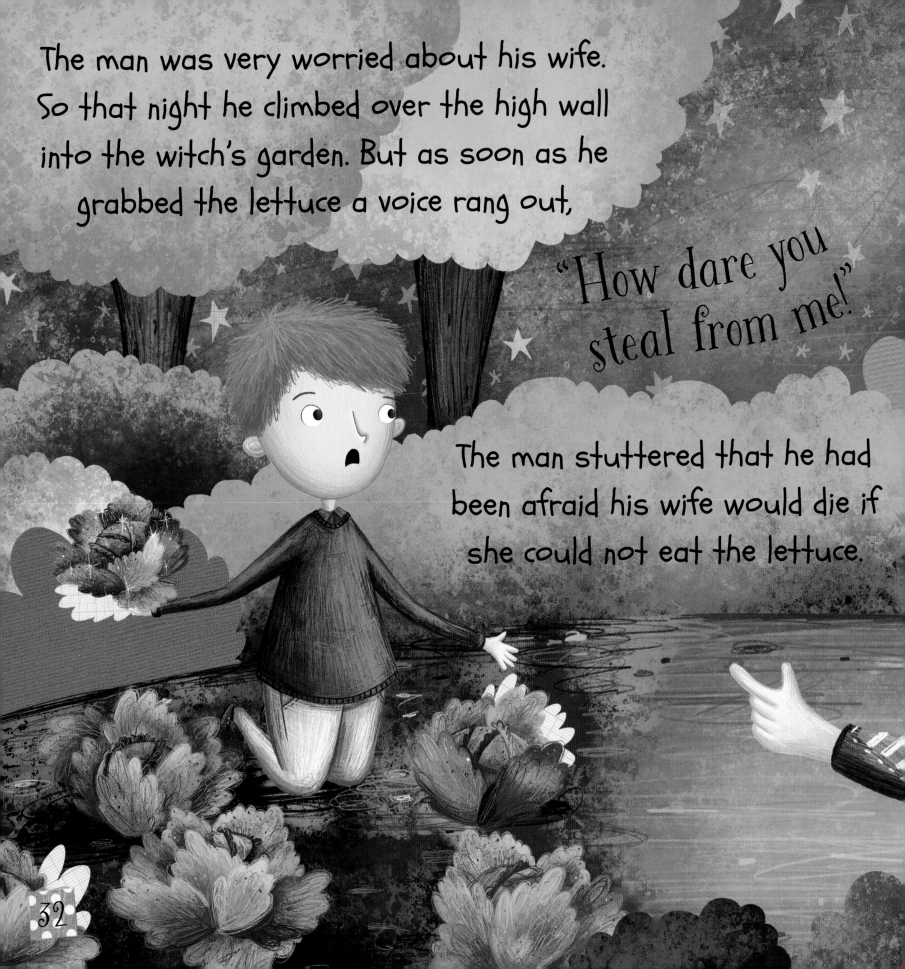

The witch thought this over. "If your wife will die without it, you may take as much of it as you like.

"In return you must give me your child when it is born. I shall be a mother to it."

33

In his panic the man agreed. He returned to his wife and sadly told her of his promise.

The couple were heartbroken, but they could think of no way out of the bargain.

A few months later their baby – a little girl – was born. The witch appeared at once, and took the child away with her.

35

The witch named the baby Rapunzel. They lived in a magic tower deep in a forest. It had no stairs or door – only a single window at the very top.

Rapunzel grew into a lovely girl, with long, thick hair. As the years passed, it grew longer... and longer.

It grew so long that instead of using magic to get into the tower, the witch could just call,

"Rapunzel, Rapunzel, let down your hair."

Rapunzel would hang her braid out of the window and the witch would climb up it.

37

One day a prince was riding through the
forest when he heard beautiful singing.
He followed it, and found the tower.

When he saw the witch,
the prince hid. He heard
her call, saw the braid
tumble down and watched
her climb up.

The prince waited for the witch to leave,
and then did his best to copy the call.

"Rapunzel, Rapunzel,
let down your hair."

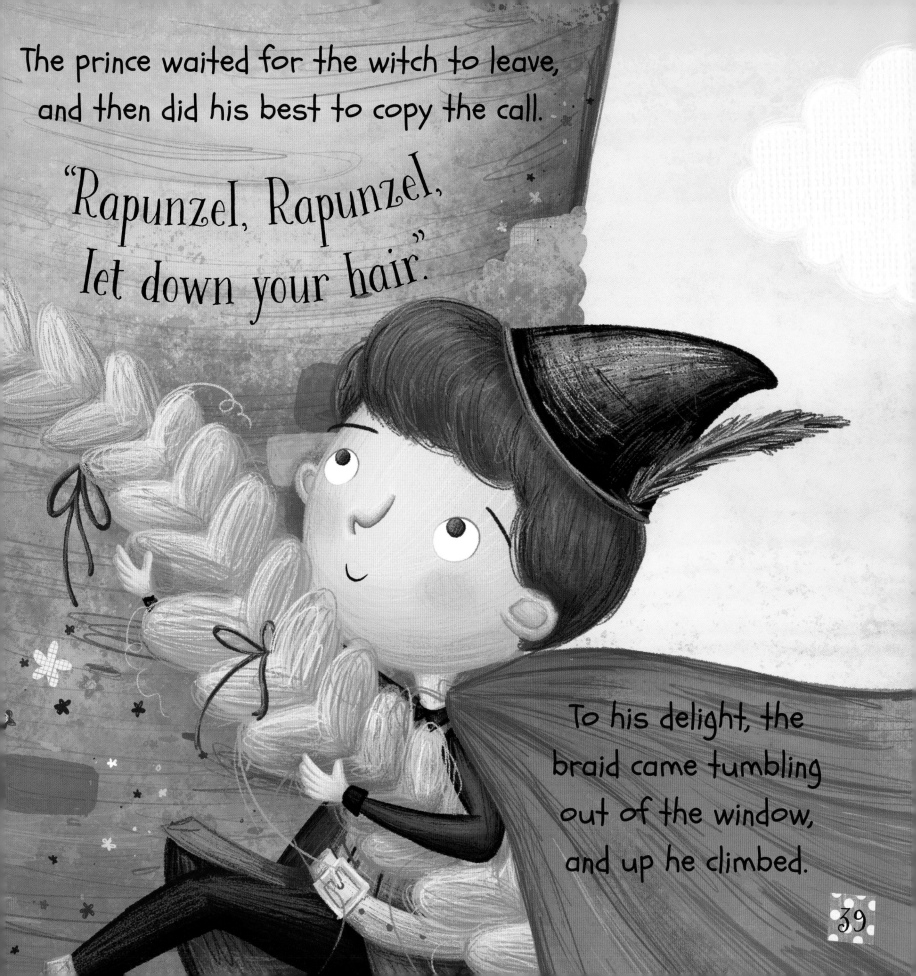

To his delight, the
braid came tumbling
out of the window,
and up he climbed.

39

At first Rapunzel was scared, but the prince was so kind that she quickly lost her fears. She told him of her lonely life in the tower.

"I must escape!" she told him.

The prince agreed to come back the next evening with a rope so they could escape together.

41

But when the witch returned she spotted a flower that the prince had given to Rapunzel. She knew at once that someone had been in the tower.

She cut off Rapunzel's braid and cast a spell that sent Rapunzel to faraway mountains.

When evening came, the witch heard the prince calling from the bottom of the tower.

She let down the braid...

...and as the prince reached the window she cast her spell.

43

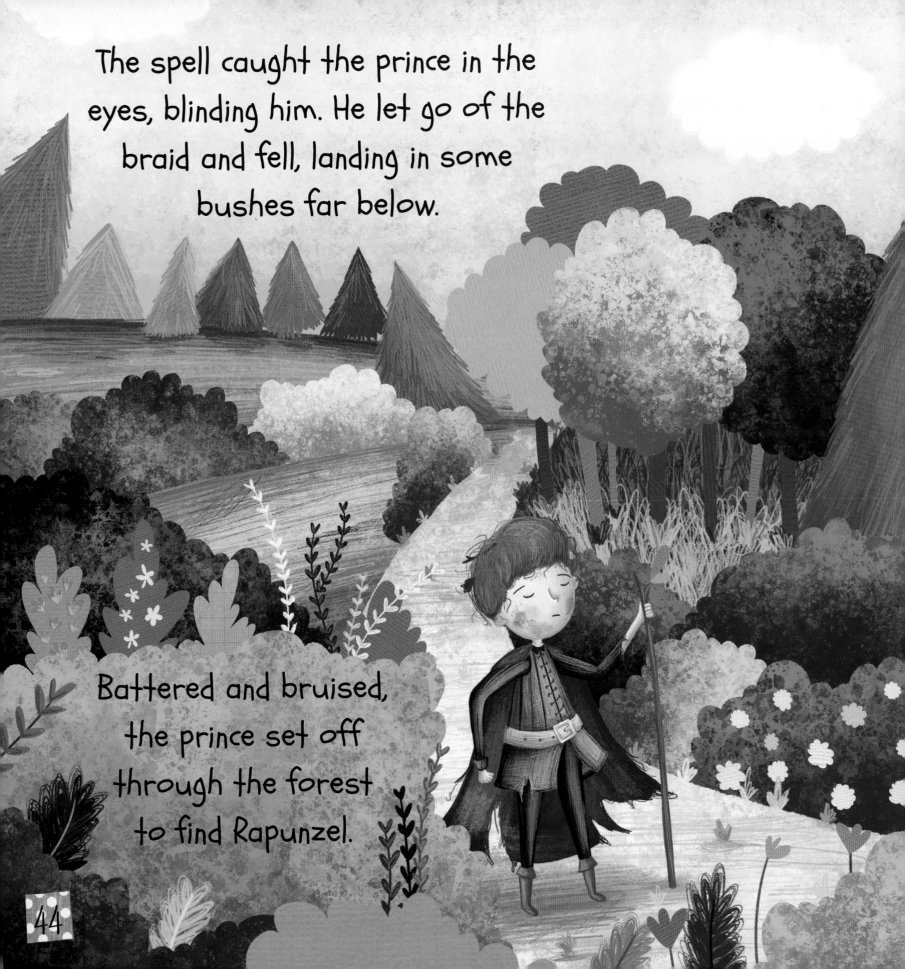

The spell caught the prince in the eyes, blinding him. He let go of the braid and fell, landing in some bushes far below.

Battered and bruised, the prince set off through the forest to find Rapunzel.

44

Behind him he heard a crumbling, creaking sound. The witch's anger had caused the tower to crack.

It tumbled to the ground – and that was the end of her.

One day, after many miles of walking, the prince heard a faint voice singing on the wind, and he followed it.

He came to a little house set among the mountains. It was here that the singing was coming from.

46

It was Rapunzel's voice the prince could hear!
Her tears of joy at the sight of him fell on the
prince's eyes and he found that he could see again.

The pair set off together
to the prince's castle.

Rapunzel's parents came to the wedding and it was a day of great joy. And they all lived happily together ever after.

Hooray!

Beauty and the Beast

Once upon a time, a wealthy merchant lived in a fine house with his daughter.

She was clever and kind and she loved to read.

Everybody called her 'Beauty'.

But one day their luck changed. Their fine house was destroyed in a fire.

Then they heard that their trading ship had been wrecked at sea.

52

Beauty and her father had to move to an old cottage in the middle of a deep, dark forest.

53

Beauty had to work hard to make
the cottage a nice place to live.

But she was brave
and cheerful and she
set to work.

One day her father set off to sell some of the food they had grown. He asked Beauty what she would like him to get her from town.

"Just a rose please, Dad," Beauty replied.

55

On his way home, Beauty's father was caught in a terrible storm. He was soon lost in the forest.

CRASH!

As night fell he came to an old castle.

The door was open, but no one was at home. He crept inside and went to sleep.

In the morning Beauty's father went into
the garden to pick a rose for his daughter.

"THIEF!"
roared a voice.

From out
of a shadow
stepped...
a *beast*.

Beauty was sad
and a bit scared, but
she tried to make
the best of it.

"It will be such an
adventure, Dad,"
she said. She set
off at once.

When she arrived at the castle, Beauty decided to explore. She saw a door marked 'Beauty's room'.

Inside was a lovely soft bed, and shelf after shelf of books! Perhaps the castle's owner might not be as cruel as he seemed.

61

That evening Beauty found a delicious meal waiting for her in the dining room. As she ate the last bite, the beast entered the room.

Though she was afraid, Beauty said thank you for her lovely room, and the books.

The beast looked pleased, and told her that everything in the castle was hers to do with as she wished.

63

Many weeks passed.
Beauty spent her
days reading.

Sometimes
she walked in
the gardens, and the
beast would join her.

They ate dinner together each night. Beauty enjoyed talking to the beast, and looked forward to seeing him.

But she still missed her father terribly.

65

One day Beauty told the beast that she was worried about her father.

The beast gave her a magic mirror.

The mirror showed Beauty her father. He looked lonely and frail.

The beast agreed Beauty should go and look after him for a week.

"I've missed you so much!"

Beauty's father was overjoyed to see her.

At the end of the week, Beauty's father begged her to stay a little longer.

Beauty agreed, but that night she had a strange, sad dream.

She saw the Beast lying still in the castle gardens.

68

Somehow she knew he was dying. She felt like her heart was breaking.

As soon as Beauty awoke from her dream she set out for the castle.

She went straight to the rose garden and found the beast lying there, quite still.

The beast whispered, "I thought you had forgotten me. Now I have seen you, I can die happy."

"No!" Beauty cried. "Don't leave me!"

"I love you."

At these words the beast vanished...
And a prince appeared in his place!

71

He had been cursed to be a beast until someone could look beyond his appearance and **fall in love with him.**

Hooray!

The two were **happy together** for the rest of their days.

The Frog Prince

Once, there lived a princess called Molly, who lived in a grand castle.

74

Every day, Princess Molly walked into the woods to play catch with her golden ball.

Her favourite spot was near a well.

One day, Molly was playing catch as usual. But she missed the ball and it bounced into the well with a **splash**.

The princess peered into
the well and wailed.
"Don't upset yourself,"
said a croaky voice.
"I can get your ball back."

77

Then a **frog** jumped onto the edge of the well. "Really?" Molly asked. "Yes," replied the frog. "But what will you give me, if I do?"

"Oh, anything," said Molly. "Then promise that we will be best friends, and let me eat from your golden plate, and sleep on your pillow," said the frog.

"Yes, yes," agreed the princess. "I promise."

So the frog **jumped** into the well. After a minute or two, he reappeared with the ball. The princess was thrilled!

80

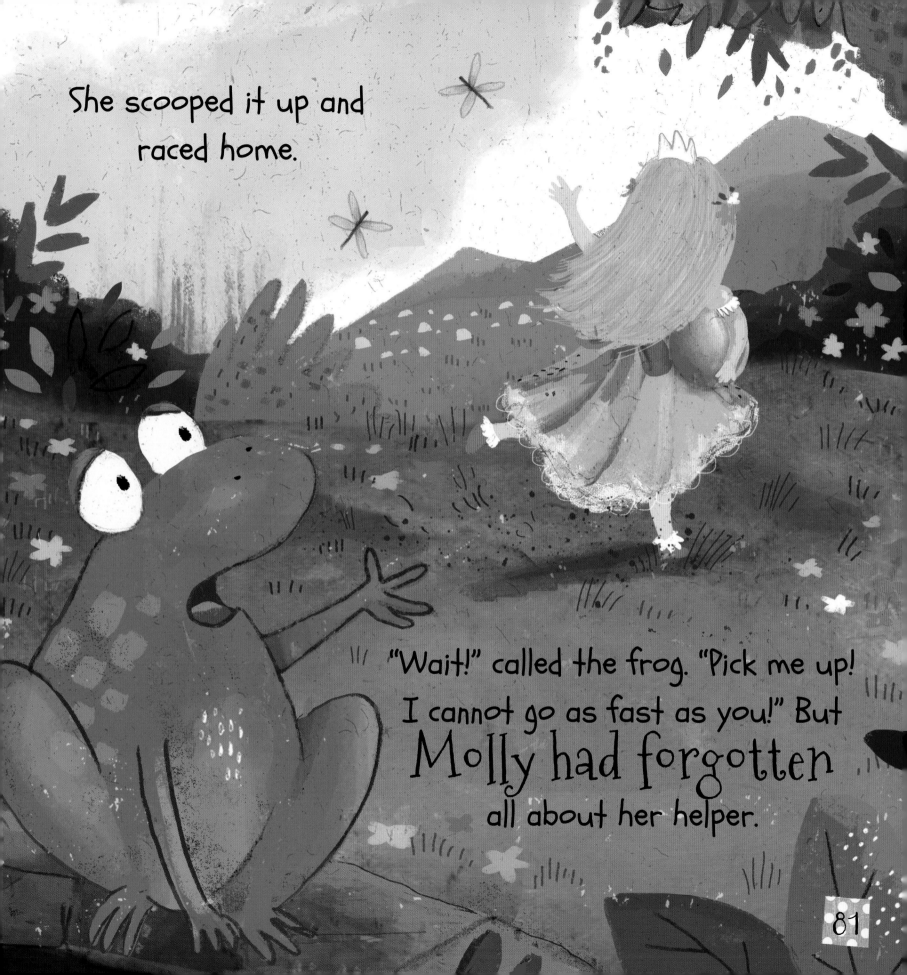

She scooped it up and raced home.

"Wait!" called the frog. "Pick me up! I cannot go as fast as you!" But Molly had forgotten all about her helper.

81

That evening, when Molly was eating dinner, there came a
splish, splash, splish, splash along the hallway.

82

Then there was a knock at the door and a voice cried,

"Princess, let me in!"

Molly opened the door to see the frog. He jumped into her arms.

83

The king asked,
"Who is it Molly?"
"It's a horrid frog," she
said, and explained what had
happened at the well that day.

"Princess, remember your promise!" croaked the frog.

The king said, "You must keep your promise, Molly." So she helped the frog onto the table, then glared at him.

85

Once the frog was on the table he said, "Now push your plate nearer so we can eat together." Molly did as he asked.

The frog munched his way through three courses while Molly barely ate a thing. At last the frog was full.

'Delicious!'

The frog yawned. "I'm tired, please put me to bed." Molly scowled, but carried him upstairs. The frog hopped up to her bedside, croaking, "Let me sleep on your pillow."

The princess groaned, but let the frog leap onto the pillow. And there he slept until the light of day, when he hopped down and out of the palace.

"ZZZZZZ!"

89

The same thing happened the following day, and the princess had to let the frog eat from her plate and sleep on her pillow. Again he left when dawn broke.

On the third day, the princess looked forward to seeing the frog. His jokes made her laugh. Once again he slept on the princess's pillow.

91

When Molly awoke the next morning, she saw a prince with kind eyes standing beside her bed. "Who are you?" asked Molly.

The prince said how a witch had enchanted him to be a frog. Molly broke the spell by keeping her promise.

"You do still look a bit like a frog!" she said.

Molly and Prince Toby became best friends. They saw each other a lot. Their favourite game was basketball, using the golden ball of course.

94

Then one day, when they were grown-up, Toby asked Molly to **marry** him. Of course she said yes.

After the wedding, they set off for Toby's kingdom in a golden carriage, with crowds cheering along the way. They lived happily ever after.

Hooray!